D0604350

# YUSE
## The Bully & the Bear

A story by John Washakie
Illustrated by Jon Cox

Published by Painted Pony, Inc. in association with the State of Wyoming

Printed by Global Interprint, Inc.
First Edition

ISBN - 0-9759806-0-2

Special thanks to:

Ft. Washakie Elementary School, students, faculty and administration
Jeston Edmo, Andrew Herrald, Derek Blackburn, Fox Ware
Quinn Carroll
The Wyoming Department of Education
The Wind River Development Fund

Translations and captions by Kathy Shoyo Standing Rock

Story adapted by Barbara Snyder
Edited by Linda Stoval

www.paintedponyinc.com

Dear Children,

Please accept this book as a gift to you from the people of Wyoming.

This story is a piece of wisdom passed from the Shoshone people to their children for many, many years. It is a legend of the Shoshone tribe about a boy who lived here long, long ago. This story is a part of Wyoming's history, and wherever you live, from Cheyenne to Jackson, from Evanston to Fort Washakie, it is a part of your history too.

This book shares the blessing of the language of the Shoshone people, who have been proud to call this land their home for hundreds of years. I hope you take the time to learn these words, and to use them when you can.

Many hearts and hands have prepared this book for you and there are many people to thank: The ancestors and storytellers of the tribe, the author, the illustrator, the translator and many others.

When we are given a gift, we often wish to express our thanks. The best way you can thank those who gave you this book is to read it again and again. I am sure you will be glad to do this, for a book is a gift that lives every time you open it.

Your friend,

Trent Blankenship
Superintendent of Public Instruction

FORWARD

For many years I have felt there has been an omission in the education of our young Wyoming citizens. I am a lifelong resident of Wyoming and an enrolled member of the Shoshone Tribe located on the Wind River Reservation. With 12 years experience in the Wyoming legislature and 25 years at Central Wyoming College, I have long hoped that my three daughters and now my six grandchildren would be exposed to Indian culture in their classrooms.

The culture and legends from the Native people have an incredible message that can assist both Indian and non-Indian in understanding life.

This book is, in my opinion, a beginning and I applaud John Washakie, whom I call my friend, for his commitment and dedication to providing others an opportunity to hear the legend his Grandma Josie now gives to children of all ages. I think it is extremely important to have the continued support of the Wyoming Department of Education in achieving this goal of bringing rich, Native culture to the classroom.

Scott Ratliff

Yuse did not like the arrow throwing game. One boy would throw the first arrow, then each boy threw his arrow, trying to come as close to the first arrow as he could. If your arrow was closest, you won. Yuse had never won.

*Hoo pa dag du da wo da ku*

It wasn't because his arrows were bad. His uncle had taught him to make good, straight arrows. It wasn't because he didn't try; he tried his best. All the other boys his age were bigger and stronger. He was short and fat.

Now it was his turn. He threw the arrow as hard and as straight as he could. He watched it soar, hoping he could come close, but his arrow fell far behind the others.
His stomach churned as the other boys laughed and the camp bully yelled, "You are too weak to ever be a warrior. You will have to stay in camp and help the women!"

Yuse ran from them and went to his favorite spot on a hill overlooking the whole camp. He sat in the shade of a large tree, out of the blistering sun.

*You va yi guy he yaif*

The valley below was peaceful with the river gently flowing beside the camp. The trees were still green with just a hint of gold and yellow against the faint outline of the mountain. The nights were getting cooler and Yuse knew winter would not be far away. The adults were busy preparing for the winter, some drying meat and others gathering berries.

Yuse came to this favorite spot to be alone and think. He had lost the arrow game - again. He thought of the time when he got so angry he charged the bully, but was wrestled to the ground and embarrassed.

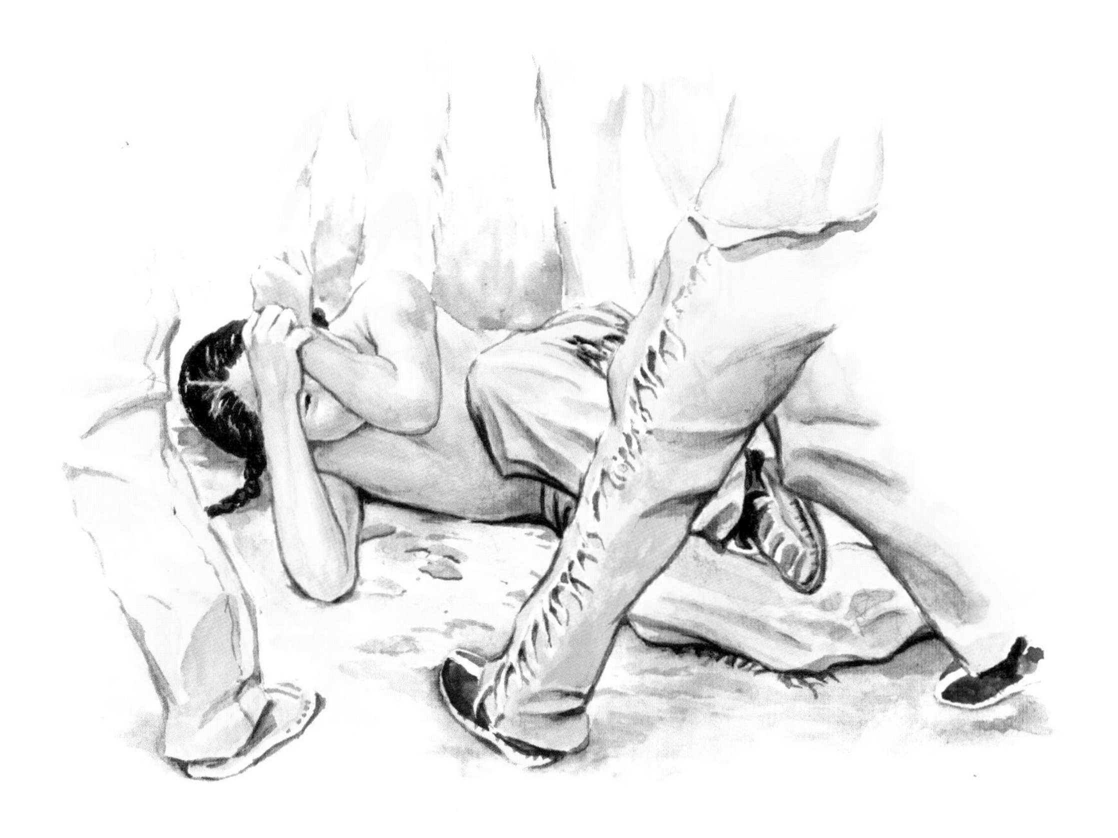

Another time, he had challenged the bully to a foot race, but he lost that, too. The other boys had laughed as he limped away. Alone here, under his favorite tree, Yuse hung his head in shame at the memories.

'Uncle says these things will change as I get older,' Yuse thought. 'Maybe so, but I wonder if I will ever be a brave warrior.'
"Tomorrow, when I am with Uncle, I will talk about this problem," Yuse said to himself.

*Na zee goo wa po nie*

Before daylight the next morning, Yuse ran to meet Uncle for a hunting trip. Yuse scrambled to keep up as they climbed high above the valley camp on the north rim of Coyote Basin. Yuse had gone with Uncle a few times before and liked being with him. He felt big and strong beside Uncle and knew that Uncle trusted him to help with the hunting. "Uncle, I am happy to go with you today," Yuse whispered. Uncle smiled in agreement.

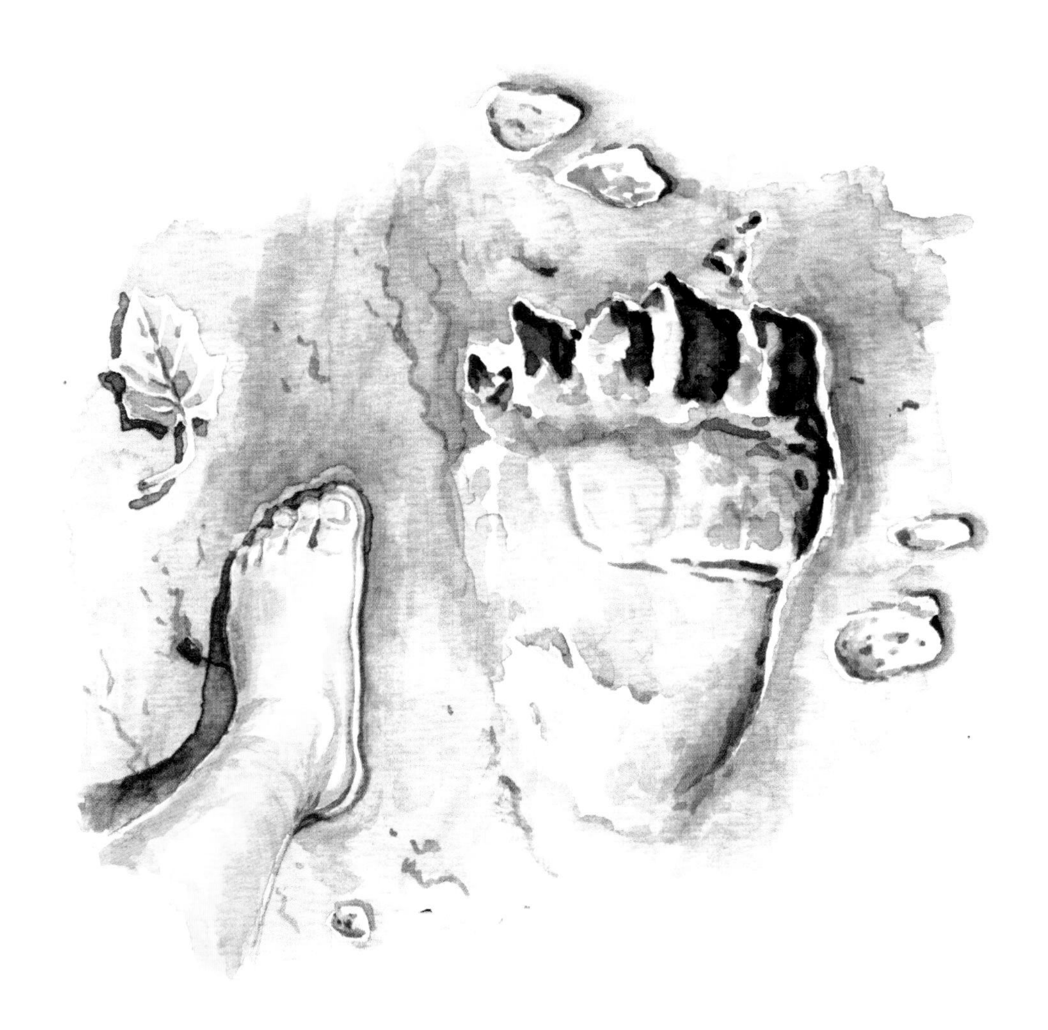

Just as the sun came over the mountain, a very old bear ambled slowly down the game trail on the other side of the valley. Uncle stopped and Yuse followed his gaze to the old bear. They sat down to watch the old bear's descent. He plodded along the game trail that led to a creek on the valley floor. It was a long way, but the old bear was thirsty and determined to get his daily drink.

*Yuse agwi nu wid*

Uncle quietly explained, "The old bear filled his belly with berries and meat yesterday. Because he is old and the creek is far away, he will drink only once a day. His teeth are very bad and he can no longer hunt and kill his own meat. He must eat soft, rotten meat of animals killed by others."

*U koo swanz-eke u goo zand dis*

The old bear took a long drink then slowly made his way back up the mountain trail. It was a good thing to see at this safe distance. For some reason, this bear reminded Yuse of his problems with the bully back at camp. He wanted to ask Uncle about his problem, but decided to wait.

In the afternoon sun, Uncle spotted tracks in the soft earth. They followed the tracks only a short distance before Uncle put his hand up signaling Yuse to stop. Yuse's heart beat fast when he spotted the big mule deer. Instantly, each pulled an arrow from his quiver and took careful aim.

'Uncle is a great hunter and I am good, too, but sometimes arrows miss,' Yuse thought. Just as they released their arrows, the deer's head came up, and he looked straight at them. For a moment Yuse felt sorry for the deer, but he knew his family needed this meat to live.

The deer seemed to fall in slow motion. They ran swiftly to the deer to make sure it was dead.

"Your aim was good. Let us quickly and quietly clean the deer," Uncle said.

Yuse smiled and felt proud. Because he had done this many times, Yuse was a big help to Uncle and they soon finished. They were both hungry, so they ate a few choice pieces of meat they had set aside for themselves. After eating, they sat under a big shade tree and rested before the long, hard trip back to camp.

*Yuse zand do hondt*

Yuse thought this was a good time to talk with Uncle about his problem with the bully.
"Uncle, I'm not very good at the arrow throwing game. I use our good, straight arrows, I try my hardest, but I never win. Most times, I don't even get my arrow close. The other boys laugh at me, and the biggest boy in camp bullies me. Then the others laugh louder. I wish I were tall and strong so I could challenge him!" Yuse said.

As always, Uncle listened and gave good advice.
"Yuse, you are good at many things," he explained, "You are a good boy and a great student. You already know the ways of the animals, and you hunted and killed this deer for your family." Yuse smiled and felt better.

Uncle went on, "Don't worry about your size. Boys grow at different times. Your father and grandfather were strong, brave warriors. You will be strong when you are grown. You will not always lose in the arrow throwing game. Now you are building skills that will help you the rest of your life. Bravery does not come from size; it comes from how well you use your head. Remember, Yuse, think before you speak."

Yuse would think about Uncle's advice later. Carrying the deer and keeping pace with Uncle's long strides was hard work. Yuse was tired, but excited to show his family the hunting success. At last he saw the light of their campfires and his pain and tiredness disappeared.

Yuse sat straight and tall as his father told the family about his success as a hunter.

"Yuse will be a great warrior. Someday our tribe will tell stories about his greatness." Yuse was filled with pride as his family looked at him and smiled.

*Ma na warah su wa zand nis ingund zand duwand*

Long after the campfire had died out, Yuse lay in bed thinking about his day. He thought about the old bear and the deer. He thought about the bully, and thought about what his father and uncle had said about him. He was determined to try harder and gain the respect of the other boys.

He quietly whispered to himself, "Tomorrow, I will play the arrow game with the bully and his friends, and this time I will win! If he beats me up, I will land a few hits of my own!"

*Ma wand nasu tand*

As the first rays of sun came peeking over the mountaintops, Yuse got up. Wrapped in his blanket, he joined his father in singing until the sun was full in the early morning sky. Then they said a prayer. His father found a comfortable seat on a log with his friends and Yuse wandered back to camp where his mother was cooking the morning meal. Yuse liked his mother's cooking, but this morning he was careful not to eat too much.

Gathering his arrows, he felt good about his meal; for once, he was not too full. With arrows in hand, he went to the open space in the center of the camp. He knew the other boys would come to play. One by one they arrived, but the bully arrived last. As he walked by Yuse, he looked down on him and laughed. Yuse held his tongue.

Suddenly, the game was on! The bully threw the target arrow. Yuse took his place in line and watched as another boy's arrow came close to the target. In turn, each boy threw hard and came close to the target. When Yuse's turn finally came, he was nervous. He took careful aim and threw his arrow as hard as he could. He watched it soar, holding his breath and hoping to hit the target. It landed far from the other arrows.

The bully laughed and shouted, "You will never be a warrior or a great hunter. You're not even strong enough to throw a little arrow!"

Yuse wanted to charge him, knock him to the ground, and punch him. But he heard Uncle's words," Think before you speak." He stood in silence and looked at the bully.

Yuse kept his face blank. And that confused and angered the bully because he could not tell what Yuse was thinking. The bully quickly changed the game to wrestling.
Pointing at Yuse he shouted, "I challenge you!" Yuse did not want to wrestle, but he did not want to run away either. He would not back down! He stood his ground. The bully moved in fast, before Yuse had time to think. He was big and strong, much bigger than Yuse, and quickly bloodied Yuse's nose. Still Yuse stood his ground. He looked at the bully and did not cry.

*Yuse ga na su-n tade ga ma de andt*

This made the bully very angry. "You are a weakling! You will never be brave. When our enemies attack, you will hide with the little children!" he screamed.

*Yuse sa du hoop mawite en dagwad gunt*

Yuse listened, careful not to show his feelings. He wanted to yell at the bully and hit him with his fist, but now he understood Uncle's advice. Speaking clearly and slowly Yuse said, "So, you think I am not brave. I challenge you to do what I do."

*Ma wa a zu tandt*

The bully laughed and taunted, "What can you do that I cannot do?"

Yuse replied, "Meet me high on the north slope before sunrise tomorrow, and we will see if you can do what I do!" The bully stared and stammered, "You are weak and..."

But Yuse was walking away - tall and proud. Some of the boys were following Yuse, asking questions, "What are you going to do, Yuse?" "You cannot beat the bully." "How can you beat him at anything?" "He is much bigger and stronger than you are." "What are you going to do?"

Yuse turned and spoke softly, "I will not say. Come if you want. You can be our witnesses."

*Dee ve zand ma zu wan zee ma gu gundt*

The next morning Yuse woke early and left camp by himself. He waited patiently on the north slope for the bully. Soon he heard the bully and his friends making their way up the trail. As they approached several ran ahead and asked, "What are you going to do?" "How can you beat the bully at anything? You are too short and fat." "Tell us what you have planned."

Yuse waited patiently until they quieted down. "Sit and watch," he said.

Just as the sun cast its first rays over the valley, Yuse quickly walked to the animal trail. His heart beat fast. He felt scared and excited at the same time. He stepped onto the trail, dropped to his knees, and lowered himself face down in the dirt. The other boys exchanged quiet, doubting looks. The bully had a smirk on his face.

Time stood still. It seemed like hours, but it was only a few minutes until the old bear came down the animal trail. When he spotted Yuse he stopped and sniffed the air. The bear was only a few feet away! Yuse could hear him growling and pawing the ground right by his head. He lay as still as he could, but his heart sounded like a drum in his chest. He wondered if the bear could hear it. He wanted to get up and run away, but if he ran now, he might always run from danger. He would face the old bear and the bully at the same time.

'The bear is thirsty, not hungry,' he thought. He felt the old bear come closer. Yuse peeked from small slits in his closed eyes and saw the bear's big paws and sharp nails. His big wet nose was cold as it sniffed around his body.

Yuse did not move a muscle.

The boys could not believe their eyes. Sure that Yuse was going to be killed and eaten by the bear, they watched in scared silence.

Just when Yuse thought he could not hold his breath one second longer, the old bear stepped over him and continued down the trail. Yuse slowly let the air out of his lungs. He was half way through. He signaled the others to stay quiet.
The old bear went to the creek and drank his fill. As he slowly ambled back up the trail, Yuse knew he must repeat his brave stunt. He lay perfectly still. The bear's cold nose tickled his feet and Yuse fought hard to stay still. The bear's breath traveled up his bare legs, over his rump, and up his back.
'I hope that Uncle is right and this old bear is not hungry,' Yuse thought, still not moving a muscle. Slowly, the old bear turned his rear to Yuse, and began covering him up. He threw dirt through his back legs with his front paws.

'Uncle was right! The old bear's teeth are soft. He is covering me up to eat in a few days when my flesh would be softer and easier to eat!' Yuse thought.

After the bear created a huge cloud of dust, Yuse jumped up and kicked that old bear as hard as he could in his big rear. The old bear was so shocked, he ran up the hill as fast as his old legs would carry him and never looked back.

*Agwai du wa va du cun na wa nu keend*

The boys erupted in laughter and excitement. With a grin on his face, Yuse walked toward them. "You are the bravest boy in the whole camp!" Weren't you scared he would eat you?" "How could you kick him like that?" they shouted.

Yuse looked right at the bully and said quietly, "Tomorrow, it is your turn."

The bully did not know what to say. He was not going to lay in the trail tomorrow or ever.
He tried an excuse, "You are crazy, Yuse! I am big and strong. The bear would much rather eat me than you."
The bully knew from the boys' faces that his bluff was not working. In fear and embarrassment he said to Yuse, "I do not accept your challenge." Then he turned and jogged back to camp by himself.

*Sud nadendt gashwand bume da ta gendt*

The other boys gathered around Yuse. Again they all spoke at once: "You are so brave," "Were you scared?" "How did you know the bear would not eat you?" "You are so smart!"

*Sud da qu hundt, su gah qua-qee qundt*

Yuse sat in his favorite spot under the big tree high on the hill. He could see his whole camp.
"I have stood up to a big bear and a bully and I feel different now. I feel stronger and better," he said proudly to himself. His life was not the same.

The bully no longer bothered him and the other boys always asked him to play in their games. He even won once in a while!

Yuse was so glad he had faced the bully in his own way. He smiled, remembering Uncle's words, "Bravery does not come from size; it comes from how well you use your head."

## Glossary

| Shoshone Word | English Word |
|---|---|
| 1. du we u pah | boy |
| 2. na dendt gash wandt | bully |
| 3. hoop a gah ma-wa dim mead | arrow |
| 4. way-gee-guy | camp |
| 5. un-guy | teepee |
| 6. a-gu-wi | bear |
| 7. newa-donzee up (enga don-zee-up) | Indian Paintbrush |
| 8. doya donzee up | Mountain Lupine (the flower) |
| 9. oh sum bado | learn |
| 10. e guh zand ma wa som ma dug | think |
| 11. bah | water |
| 12. boy-ha vid | trail |
| 13. be ah | mom |
| 14. a dah | uncle |
| 15. a pah | dad |
| 16. be ah qee-ah | eagle |
| 17. qu wee ah-see-ump | feather |

Illustration Captions

Page 8. *Hoo pa dag du da wo da ku*
The game of arrows

Page 12. *You va yi guy he yaif*
Yuse's camp in the early fall

Page 15. *Na zee goo wa po nie*
Yuse's Uncle is a wise teacher

Page 17. *Yuse agwi nu wid*
Yuse learns about this bear and how it lives

Page 18. *U koo swanz-eke u goo zand dis*
Learning to think is a good lesson

Page 21. *Yuse zand do hondt*
Yuse is a good hunter

Page 23. *Ma na warah su wa zand nis ingund zand duwand*
Yuse's family is grateful that he is a good hunter.

Page 26. *Ma wand nasu tand*
Yuse and his father pray

Page 29. *Yuse ga na su-n tade ga ma de andt*
Yuse is still brave even when hurt by the bully

Page 30. *Yuse sa du hoop mawite en dagwad gunt*
Yuse confronts the bully

Page 31. *Ma wa a zu tandt*
Yuse challenges the bully to show bravery

Page 33. *Dee ve zand ma zu wan zee ma gu gundt*
Yuse comes up with a good plan to beat the bully

Page 37. *Agwai du wa va du cun na wa nu keend*
The bear is tricked and runs away

Page 38. *Sud nadendt gashwand bume da ta gendt*
The bully is afraid to do what Yuse did

Page 40. *Sud da qu hundt, su gah qua-qee qundt*
After defeating the bully, Yuse becomes a great leader

This book is dedicated to Josephine Trehero Washakie,
known to all as "Gramma Josie".

John Washakie

John R. Washakie
Spouse: Bonnie J.
Children: Tonya, Joe, Candace
Grandchildren: Kyle, Kristen, Kayle, Chase, Kathy,
Wekota, Hailey, Jackie, Yvonne,
Kailyn, Kanani, Kenny, Keeley
Born: Fort Washakie, Wyoming

Before he started writing, he spent 18 years on the Eastern Shoshone Business Council. While on the Council, he made numerous presentations to the House of Representatives and Senate Select Committee on Indian Affairs. He was appointed by 3 different Department of Interior Secretaries to serve on several national committees to address issues from Reorganization of the Bureau of Indian Affairs to Energy policy. He is the great grandson of Chief Washakie whose statue was recently placed in the rotunda of the U.S. Capitol. He earned a B. A. in History from the University of Wyoming. He is a veteran of the Vietnam War. He claims to be an average writer and just a good listener when his grandmother, uncles, or anyone else told stories. With the tradition of storytelling being almost gone, John decided he must use the new technologies of computers, printing and publishing to save these stories so that they would once again be passed on.

Jon T. Cox

I grew up in Cheyenne, Wyoming and graduated from East High School, The University of Wyoming and most importantly, the school of life. I have had a variety of occupations and been many things in my time. I owe a great deal of these experiences, successes and strengths to my parents, sister, brother and family. My wife Tammy and my children, Kelly, Katy and Jon have allowed me to be whatever I dreamed. I love them all. From the experience of raising and contributing to a family, one learns a lot about life and the lessons it presents for passage through it. Another passion and love of mine is gardening. My wife has taught me a great deal about it and is the real gardener. I am really just the lawn boy.

One of the people who taught me other important lessons in life was Professor Victor Flach, who directed my Masters' program. He believed that we must make a record of our experiences. If we do not, then we must ask, did they ever happen? Although only a story, this book is a record and vital part of Native American culture that must not be allowed to disappear. I consider it a privilege to have been allowed to record this traditional story through my illustrations.

As for John Washakie, he is not one to talk about himself or his accomplishments. He is above all a great listener and because of that, he has learned many wonderful stories that colorfully teach life's lessons. This is one of them and if you listen well enough, you too will learn a great deal.

Jon Cox